Obinna Dick

CW00591419

George in the Magical World of Mengas

**George in the Magical
World of Mengas**
Signed by Obinna Dickson
£6:99 paid   22.3.2008

Chikaleonsenterprises Ltd story series

<u>Other books by Obinna Dickson</u>

1.   Dinosaur Quest

2.   Round the Glass Top Roof

3.   The Burglars

4.   Trix

5.   Obinna's Poems

6.   Obinna's Fairy tales

7.   Obinna's Myths and Legends

8.   Obinna's Fables

-Dedicated to my Mummy -

Special thank you to my Mother, Onuchika Dickson, for helping and guarding me in my story writing and for my little sister, Nneka and best friend, Joshua, who's imaginative plays inspired my writing. I especially wish to thank Cheryl, Ruth and Claire, my Drama teachers, at the famous Helen 'O'Grady Drama school in Stretford, who have inspired me to put into practice my acting skills. To Elaine and Martin Trimble, Special thank you for believing in me.

Published by Chikaleonsenterprises Ltd

First published 2008 - Obinna Dickson

© 2008 Chikaleonsenterprises Ltd
Address: 31 Garswood Road, Fallowfield Manchester M14 7LJ
www.obinnajdickson.com

ISBN   978-1-906 569-01-3
Retail price: £6:99

Printed in the United Kingdom
Cover illustration by Obinna Dickson
Consultant Artist: Austin Chaba
Illustrations copyright © 2008 Obinna Dickson
Typeset, printed and bound in the United Kingdom by
PD Print Ltd. 0161-367 7854

These short stories are a work of fiction. Names, characters, place and
incidents are a product of the author's imagination or used fictitiously.
Any resemblance to actual people living or dead, events or locals
is entirely coincidental.

This book belongs to:

....

....

....

....

-CONTENTS-

-CHAPTER 1-
THROUGH THE WATER

SCHOOL was boring for George, especially maths, but now it was homework time and Mr. Thornhill was handing out homework. "Today class, he said, "you are going to write an imaginary story either about yourself or a made up character".

School was about to finish and George was nearly half asleep from hard handwriting, and maths classes. But today was Friday, so he had Saturday and Sunday to relax and enjoy himself. On the way home, George was so tired that he took a short cut home; so he would get home easily and finish his homework, but he had to first cross over a very unstable bridge, which stood over a huge lake.

George was about to walk on when all of a sudden, a fox ran pass George with a rabbit in his hand. George stared at the fox with fear. George quickly ran underneath a huge dead tree to hide from the fox that he didn't notice his hat was blown away and was now floating in the water. As he walked onto a safer area of the wood, George saw some robin perching on a huge tree branch. He stopped to say 'hello' to a few of the birds and squirrels that he could see. He rested underneath the tree branches for awhile, before setting off again on his way home.

George thought to himself: I wonder whether the fishermen come here. If they do, it would truly be a terrible place to go in; at the same time he was trying to catch his hat.

Tired of trying to catch his hat, George followed a familiar route to make his way home. After a two hour long walk, he came to the Camelot Bridge. At the bridge, there was an inscription on a sign of the bridge saying "1309"; the old bridge was probably built in 1309. As George walked across the bridge he saw little ducks swimming in the water, and down the deeper end, he could hear fishermen talking of their daily hunt. He was so busy staring at the water, that he did not notice a goblin grab him from underneath the bridge.

The creature swam underneath the long river which was leading to an old abandoned farm. As the Goblin carried young George, he swam through a deep hole leading to a dark empty area but in the most sudden movement the great big goblin was attacked by a tiger shark, leaving George to sail deep down to the bottom of the sea.

As George swam under the sea, two sharks saw him and wanted him for tea. This made George shocked; because many people said that there were no sharks for miles, so George now knew he was sailing through shark territory (George lived in Cardiff). All the sharks swam towards George and scared the living day light out of him. Suddenly a shark said, "Eh Rocker! doesn't that boy look luscious?" The other shark replied, "Oh yes, good enough to eat". George fainted with fear, not because of the fact that they were going to eat him, but because of the fact that each and every one of the animals could talk. As time progressed, George grew tired and fell asleep by the river bank.

When George woke up he saw two grizzly Goblins staring at him eagerly "Please don't eat me, I beg of you" George cried "Oh shut it, we will not eat you, on the condition ……that you help my wife do the cleaning" the Goblin said cheerfully "Okay!" replied George. Mrs Goblin, showed George around the house, but was later called to do something else. In the meantime, George sat down sorrowfully waiting for more instructions. Finally Mrs. Goblin came back with a duster in her hand, made from sea weed and a lovely meal of shrimp and chicken from the farm near by. She gave George the brush. Goblin's wife excused herself, while she began to prepare Mr. Goblin's meal. Mr. Goblin on the other hand, protected the ancient bridge from trespassers, by making sure that no trespassers crossed the ancient bridge without his say so.

There was a tremendous bang at the door and there stood Octopus, shark, crocodile, jellyfish, angler fish, eel, goldfish, alligator, lobster and spider crab. "What on earth do you want?" the goblins wife asked them and they replied, "We want your land dweller". George swam from behind a cactus plant taking out prickles from his legs and arms "Me?" he shouted "Yes, you!" they all said. Two hours later Mr. Goblin came back screaming 'Where is that boy George! Whom I found at Mrs. Octopus's house?'

George was so afraid of the Goblins, in search of a hiding place, he slowly walked into a big sea mansion that was spotless and clean. George was bemused, that Mr & Mrs. Goblin wanted him to clean a spotless house? Why on earth were they asking him to tidy a house if it was already clean? "Why do you want me to help you, when your house is extraordinarily clean?" asked George "I have kids and they mess this house up replied Mrs Goblin. Very well, go and give Mrs Octopus a hand, her house needs tidying up! "Anyway, you're here to work, not to ask questions" replied Mrs. Octopus handing him out a long list and then she went off. George looked at it plainly and this is what it said:

List

Give all my kids tea.

Clean house except the special Room which must not be entered

Cook me some shark and seahorse Cocktail (in the sack by the edge of table)

And Dust the seaweed in my back garden.

The next few days were tough for young George, for the children were rude and endlessly messed up the house. The children blamed George for the clutters around the house and threatened George not to tell or they would squirt ink at him, and then strangle him with their tentacles. When Mrs. Octopus had come back from the ink factory, she opened the door and went into the parlour in shock! In an angry outburst "WHO ON EARTH

DIRTIED MY HOUSE?" boomed Mrs. Octopus at the top of her voice "It was George!" chorused the two little octopuses. George just stood there, waiting for Mrs. Octopus to say something to him "Young man, you have caused a lot of trouble and we shall give you to the sharks, if you do it again!". Mrs. Octopus announced she was going to the market, but really she was hiding behind a cactus and caught eye of every thing: One octopus poured raspberries over the floor and another threw apples and seaweed around the yard. Then they said, "IF YOU TELL YOU'LL NEVER (EVER) LIVE TO SEE THE DAYLIGHT AGAIN!!!!"

George in the Magical World of Mengas

At this point, little George was terrified, holding back tears dripping down his eyes, when suddenly, Mrs. Octopus appeared "Oh, will he now?" she shouted to her naughty children. She then listened to the boys' excuses and then covered their mouth "Land dweller" she announced "you are free to leave". As George swam for freedom he could hear screaming and whipping from Mrs. Octopus's house. George was about to swim upland but four envious sharks jumped rapidly in front of him and tried to eat him, but George bounced away from his position and they banged into a rock.

George was struggling on to land, but before he managed to make it, a bird swooped down and picked him up. While he was held captive by the angry looking crane, he realised he was heading towards a forest and he smelled the lovely smell of homemade apple pie and some lovely muffins.

-CHAPTER 2-
SIR ROBINSON MAKASWELL OF MENGAS

GEORGE WAS dropped into the forest by the Crane, but when he opened his frightened little eyes and looked around his glittering surroundings, he was now seating on top of a Siberian tiger. The tiger somehow jumped up and chased George into a glass building that was no bigger than a carriage which one rides in, to get to far places. The tiger tried to scratch the glass and break it open. Vibration from the broken glasses forced the inpatient tiger to land on his back, so George found a good opportunity to escape into another part of the building.

Twelve hours later, exhausted George had slept off inside glass castle; the castle was sound proof, so George slept soundly undisturbed, while the tiger banged on the glass from the outside. The tired tiger decided to travel to another part of the forest in search of preys. Some hours later, George opened his eyes, realising that he was still in the magical garden, George ran into a neighbouring little cottage. Suddenly he bumped into a medium sized old man with a moustache and coat of armour (including a helmet). His hair stuck out from the side of his helmet and it was ginger; his eyes were green. There was the statue of a dragon on his front door, the dragon's nose was a little bit triangular "Who on earth are you?" asked baffled George!

"Sir Robinson Makaswell, the Knight of Mengas" replied the old man, and then the knight repeated the same question back to George, " And who are you, are you new around here?" George vividly turned around, facing a table full of newly baked cakes. He replied "George. George Archwood". It appeared the knight was baking biscuits, muffins and some bread. The room was infused with the sweet smelling aroma of his baking. Hungry and, enticed by the display of chocolate cakes display, George said "Why are you cooking if you're a Knight?" The Knight, replied; "It's my hobby, my boy... Now you must be hungry, after being chased by the Tiger? Have some cakes to eat" Sir Robinson

Makeswell asked George to help himself to some cakes. "Where am I?" asked George "Why, you are in Mengas".

George grabbed a chocolate cake from the table and began to chew it, when all of a sudden he heard a growling and a familiar moaning coming from the glass building. Sir Robinson laughed at George when he revealed that the Tiger belonged to a fox. "You little Puskins, there is no boy in the glass building". (Puskins was the name of the tiger "That tiger tried to eat me" George said "Oh he was not. Anyone he sees he chases them and licks them and Pablo fox is his owner, a very experienced man in animals".

George tucked into a bun and then he ate a sausage "Do not eat all of it or there will be none left for the King's Christmas party" ordered Sir Robinson, George looked up at Sir Robinson a little bit puzzled "What party?" he said curiously and Sir Robinson gave him a letter which read:

"My royal subjects,

----As one being a King who has a heart of lovingness I send this letter to tell you on Tuesday 28th December, you and one or two friends are invited to my Christmas party. After a very special meeting in the Cathedral, we shall sing carols and dance to music, play games and even better, we shall eat lovely homemade food made by you; then drink champagne and play in the snow maze before having your scrumptious Christmas pudding. And go home with presents----.

Yours Sincerely, King James.

Sir Robinson chatted away to George, and said, "I was wondering whether you could help me make a special chocolate cake with chocolate flakes and white cream with honey drizzling down it?" asked Sir Robinson, "sorry but no thanks" said George "Impostor" George, who was going to ask Sir Robinson how old he was but at the last second he remembered his parents said it was rude to ask older people their age, so he kept his mouth shut and said nothing.

Sir Robinson suggested to George that he could come along to the Christmas party, to meet the other members of the Magical world of Mengas. George was so thrilled that he was invited and quickly accepted his invitation. "Do you know, my boy, said Sir Robinson Makeswell, I received a second letter from my friend, Sinister Bunny; he invited me to play the "Golden Maze Challenge, with a friend or relative. Sinister Bunny is a bunny rabbit, who is ever so spoilt and brags a lot how he wins in every game and if he does not win he will be angry".

It is to play a game of golden maze" he said "you can come" he added. If you join me today, you can play against Sinister Bunny and many more people, but you can only win if you reach the end of the maze and if you cheat, you will be hanged in front of everybody. George never said no to a challenge, so he accepted. Sir Robinson Makeswell called out to his own Tiger by telling his two servants to blow their trumpets, calling on the Tiger who is the messenger to the Knight. All of a sudden, the roaring of a Tiger was heard and Richard the Horse came trotting in, followed by the Tiger. Sir Makeswell then gave them his reply letter to be delivered to his good old friend Sinister Bunny.

-CHAPTER 3-
-SINISTER BUNNY AND HIS GAMES-

IT WAS A FREEZING COLD morning, on the day of Sinister Bunny's party. Early that morning, George rested inside the cave, in preparation for the great game, while Sir Robinson Makeswell went to pick up some apples to bake more apple pies. George was left with Stalactites hovering over him. He knew he was not alone because if he was alone he would not hear hissing. He laid his rucksack on the table and went to inquire where the hissing was coming from. The hissing sounded muffled, so George knew it was coming from some rocks.

George picked up some rocks and saw a boa constructor slithering on a Clementine, "You poor thing" said George sympathetically. The snake replied "I was heading to Sinister Bunny's party and I saw a Clementine I headed straight for it but the next thing I know is that a pile of rocks fell on me; but at least I have got a Clementine". Suddenly George heard galloping of horses coming from below them, so they hid behind a rock and looked at a small creature ridding on a horse, "Is that a Pygmy?" asked George suspiciously "Yes, and she is heading for the Midnight Garden, a mysterious garden where it always snows and it is always night time.

When Sir Robinson came back they all ate some apples and then went on their journey "Do you want more apple's boys? Sinister's Bunny's speech can take up to 9 hours".

Sinister Bunny's house was very big and had a tremendous 10 floors! The house looked a little bit of Tudor style house. On the front door there was a sign saying: No Rhinoceros, dirty people who mess up and dirty things and no robbers.

George concentrated on a grocery shop saying: SINISTER BUNNY'S GROCERY' and next to it a public house called THE APPLE CRUMBLE. A small and slim bunny with a one-spectacle glass came out from the grocery shop holding a turkey. His fur was grey and he had a stubby white tail; his eye's were like a turquoise diamond, glittering on the ground; his teeth were so clean that you would think they were babies' teeth and his lips were red roses growing in heaven. "Good day to you all" he said with rather a tiny voice that brought happiness in to the snake and Goliath the horse, "Do come in I have just finished my speech" he said letting them in and then looking around for the witch.

On the very table sat some people George remembered – Mr and Mrs Goblin. Mrs Goblin was holding the same book every one else was holding 'William Bunnyspeare' "Hallo" said Mr. Goblin looking at George angrily. Anyway, they were not the only ones on the table: there was an owl, a pigeon, eighteen rabbits, five hares, a tiger, a hawk, a bull, a crocodile, a sloth, a cat, a dog, some vulture's, Australian eagles, a lion, a lioness, a hippopotamus, a bear, a polar bear, the snake, George, Sir Robinson Makaswell of Mengas and 30 panda's.

About 12 servants came in with roasted wild boar, swan, ducks, turkey and potatoes with gravy, some Christmas pudding, a Chocolate cake, a very big bowl of fruit and cream, cranberry sauce was on the table not to mention cauliflower and carrot soup with custard and dip in mince pies. "DIG IN" shouted the bunny at the top of his voice.

Two hours later a chicken walked in from the back of the gate with a turkey and a dodo "I do not remember inviting you" said Sinister Bunny angrily "We are thieves and we want your food" they ordered. Since the bunny was speechless, George interrupted "If you want his food you must win it fair and square by playing snakes and ladders" said George "The one thing the robbers did not know was that George was a champion when it came to snakes and ladders.

"What a marvellous idea but I have a better idea. Why not play Question –mania, I ask a question and if you get it right you move up a number" said Sinister Bunny pointing to a number square. And so the game began. The two robbers and George stood on number one and Sinister Bunny started to try and ask questions.

"How many hours does it take Rabbit Clause to give presents?" said Sinister with a big grin on his face "7 hours" said George, curiously starting to wonder if he was right or wrong "Correcto". For three and a half hours George answered every single bunny history question without a single era or correction made. "George is our winner, and it looks like he knows all about Bunny History" said Sinister Bunny. Overjoyed that he had won his only desire back, George smiled all he way back to the castle, however the robbers went away very angry and upset.

"Oh, its time for the King's party, we had better go and get a fancy dress" said the panda who was tapping his weary wife "I am not coming" announced George with a huge frown on his face.

CHAPTER 4
-A PARTY DRESS-

EVERYONE was so exited that they did not notice George sneak out. He ran into the old cottage and waited for the rain to stop. The cottage had lots of Chinese ornaments and an important doll made from china. Also in a room that must have been the parlour, was a huge Roman settee with a marble table and on the shelf was an outstanding amount of books, the shelves were so dusty.

"Can I help you young man?" asked an old lady with a bag of money in her hands "Emm….. I would like…….. Anything...Emm...Emm…A PARTY DRESS!" said George quite confused because he was just staying to get out of the rain "You took your time" said the old lady laughing her head off "Follow me dear" she said with a big grin on her face.
George and the lady walked up the ancient castle,

where the party was taking place. The narrow floral path was half broken; it had creaky steps which led to a small room with wardrobes full of clothes ready to be worn. On the table next to the small dirty till was a sewing kit.

"Now" said the old woman calmly. "Choose what you like, while I go and get you something yummy to eat". a Black and white Persian Cat entered into the room, through the open doors, she came to stand opposite George, staring intensely at him. George admired a lovely cowboy dress which cost 12 guineas, but on the other side of the room was a lovely prince's dress which costs 4 shillings. He did not purchase it, instead he paraded himself to other clothe hangers in search of cheaper costumes.

Later George's eye was fixed on a huge giant dress that cost 2 pounds and 1 shilling.

Soon George began to have flashes of his parents'

disapproval of him not being allowed to wear monsters costumes. He also reflected that his family would be awfully worried that he had gone for 2 days or more and he remembered that he was not allowed to wear any monster costumes.

"Maybe I can wear this to Henrietta's fancy dress party" whispered George looking at the lovely pussy cat costume. Then he paused to the sound of laughing. George went down stairs in secret and saw the old pygmy putting poison into George drink. He then realised that these creatures in the Mengas Castle planned to kill and have him for their supper.

George frantically ran up stairs, grabbed his school bag, and threw it around his neck, making sure he did not leave anything of his behind. As George rushed out in a hurry, he tripped over a suitcase and he could hear sounds of evil laughing "What is going up there?" asked the old lady "Nothing, I am just making sure I chose the right costume" lied George. George quickly opened the window, grabbing at a broomstick which he found by the window. Then he got onto it and flew out of window just in time for the old evil Pygmy could climb upstairs.

As George flew over the village on his broomstick, he could see a family of Pygmies shouting to others, calling them to catch the alien boy, who is running away from the magical Mengas castle. George confidently looked down the castle, he saw two robbers, sneaking into the house (the same that were in Sinister house), and two hours after he had flown over Sinister Bunny's house everyone was pointing at him, shouting 'Yes that is George'.

He flew over the Midnight Garden and saw a man sitting on a fountain looking at clocks. The man got up and hissed at George (probably thinking George was a one of the Pygmies.

George flew pass Sir Robinson's house, he also flew

over the rain forest and the ferocious river, George waved down at Mr. and Mrs. Goblins, who were no doubt, keeping an eye on intruders to the Magical world of Mengas, Mr and Mrs Goblin smiled and wove back at George.

George landed by the royal gate waiting for someone to assist him. Gold sparkled all over the gate like the gate in Saudi Arabia" (his father had told him that). It was shining bright and the birds might have finally come out from their nest to sing summer song to the sun. Down the alley way, stood a tiny little footstep of a mouse coming up the lane to the party (it went in the maze, the party would be over when he comes out because the maze was bigger than him).

"Are you Edward of Locksley?" asked George to the Mouse "Yes I am" he replied, so George and Edward both turned round and started talking. To make things even better, a dog came and chatted with them. The two boys now felt safe, being accompanied by the forest dog.

They got close to the river of Mengas and a very strong wind blew the Mouse's wig into the river, the mouse was dressed elegantly in Persian Satin. "My beautiful wig!!!!! Somebody save it, before it get's too wet to wear" chanted the mouse. George jumped into the river and swam and swam, until he could not swim any longer.

"I'm sinking" cried George from the top of his voice; The frightened Mouse looked on, the Dog jumped into River Mengas, to retrieve the wet wig. Soon they arrived at their destination, the dog bid them good bye until next time.

When George woke up, he was amazed to find, his mother, father, nurse and a doctor all on his bedside crying with a worried look on their faces, and the doctor calmly said in a high pitched voice "Master Archwood you nearly got pneumonia. If this dog had not found you on time! You would have been dead!" said the doctor sadly. The Doctor, asked to speak with Mr. and Mrs. Archwood in private, outside George's nursery (Victorian nursery).

Dr. Zulu advised Mr. and Mrs. Archwood to keep George in his bed for a few days. "Your son needs a lot of rest and make sure he takes his medication twice a day as prescribed". Soon after this, Dr. Zulu came back into George's room and shouted: "Young man, stay out of trouble and rest until you feel much better. I'll see you next time"! George said "Thank you" to Dr. Zulu.

Mr. and Mrs. Archwood came back into the room. Mrs. Archwood held George's hands warmly and smiled at him, while the nurse stood at the end of the bed. "You look like you could do with some food, George" said the nurse. George nodded to her in agreement. The nurse left the room, to get some food for George and left him alone in the room with Sir Robinson Makeswell smiling at him.

About the Author

Obinna Dickson, aged 10

Obinna was born in Boston, Massachusetts USA, in February 1998 to Nigerian Parents. At the time of this publication, Obinna attended Moss Park Junior School, Stretford, Manchester and was in year five. Obinna and his family live in Manchester, England. At a very young age of five, Obinna's passion for literary writing emerged from his weekly attendance at the Helen O' Grady Drama School, where he learnt to prepare plays and to art with his peers. Obinna went on to win many drama medals and child modelling career. At home, Obinna enjoys nothing more than watching his favourite Dr. WHO movies and writing personal hand written scripts and plays. This was how his quest for writing emerged to this day. In school, Obinna's favourite subjects are Literacy and History, his future aspiration is to become a Film Director and a Script Writer. Obinna's mother, Onuchika, helped kick-start his literary career by buying him a computer and scanner on his 7th birthday. Friends and family members have been amazed at Obinna's literary elevation at such a young age. We thank God for his wonderful progression in becoming a young author. Enjoy **George in the magical world of Mengas**, Obinna's first published paperback fictional story.

BOOK REVIEW

To assist the author in improving his writing career, would you be kind to complete this questionnaire and post to the publisher to: 31 Garswood Road, Fallowfield Manchester M14 7LJ

I give this book _____ out of 10 because
_____

My favourite part was
_____
_____

because
_____
_____

My least favourite part was
_____
_____

because
_____

My favourite Character was
_____
_____

because_____
_____

My least favourite character was
_____
because _____

.I _____ read this book again because
_____

My favourite time to read it is night time/ morning time/ in school/in the car because
_____
_____

ORDER FORM

To order direct from the Publisher, complete the form below:

Name:………………………………………………………………………..

Address:…………………………………………………………………….

…………………………………………………………………………………

……….………………………………………………………………………

…………………………………………………………………………………

Post code:…………………….

Send to:

Chikaleonsenterprises Publishers
'Oroma'
31 Garswood Road,
Fallowfield,
Manchester M14 7LJ

Please make cheques and postal orders payable to:
Chikaleonenterprises publishers

Please enclose a cheque or postal order to the value of the cover price, plus UK
postal cost of £2.00 per copy and 50 pence for each additional book ordered.

Overseas and USA, please add £3.99 for postal cost and
service charges.